SARA L SEN

BLAKE AND THE
RISE OF THE PHOENIX

BALBOA.
PRESS

A DIVISION OF HAY HOUSE

Balboa Press books may be ordered through booksellers or by contacting:

Balboa Press
A Division of Hay House
1663 Liberty Drive
Bloomington, IN 47403
www.balboapress.com
1 (877) 407-4847

Because of the dynamic nature of the Internet, any web addresses or links contained in this book may have changed since publication and may no longer be valid. The views expressed in this work are solely those of the author and do not necessarily reflect the views of the publisher, and the publisher hereby disclaims any responsibility for them.

The author of this book does not dispense medical advice or prescribe the use of any technique as a form of treatment for physical, emotional, or medical problems without the advice of a physician, either directly or indirectly. The intent of the author is only to offer information of a general nature to help you in your quest for emotional and spiritual well-being. In the event you use any of the information in this book for yourself, which is your constitutional right, the author and the publisher assume no responsibility for your actions.

Any people depicted in stock imagery provided by Getty Images are models, and such images are being used for illustrative purposes only. Certain stock imagery © Getty Images.

This is a work of fiction. All of the characters, names, incidents, organizations, and dialogue in this novel are either the products of the author's imagination or are used fictitiously.

Scripture taken from the King James Version of the Bible.

Print information available on the last page.

ISBN: 978-1-5043-9937-1 (sc)
ISBN: 978-1-5043-9938-8 (e)

Balboa Press rev. date: 03/01/2018

Table of Contents

BLAKE AND THE RISE OF THE PHOENIX

Characters of *Blake and the Rise of the Phoenix*

Blake, founder member of the rebel alliance, interrogated, feared, envied, and annoyed by the Foundation, was a wanted criminal of the Foundation of planets who rescued the criminals from the prison ship *The London* to acquire the ship the *Alligator* and become a leader of its crew.

Arden was a computer expert, rebel, and former jewel thief, also an icy ally of Blake aboard the *Alligator*, and later, a decision maker on the ship the *Skanda*.

Jemma was was a space pilot, friend and ally of Blake, and a crew member of the *Alligator*.

Kaali was a telepath from the planet Avon and a crew member of *The Alligator*.

Victor was a cowardly criminal known for door, safe, and joke cracking as well as being an ally of Blake. He was also a crew member of the ships the *Alligator* and the *Skanda*.

Brent was a former Foundation soldier who became an ally of Blake and a crew member aboard the *Alligator* and the *Skanda*.

Anna was a rebel known for expert fighting, who joined the crew of the *Alligator* and later the *Skanda*. Her father was personally killed by Saradan.

Sara was an expert gunfighter and former girlfriend of the original owner of the *Skanda*, who stayed as a crew member of the *Skanda* and was later joined by the former crew of the *Alligator*.

Oros was a talking computer created by earthling genius Anson, who joined the crew of the *Alligator* and later the *Skanda*, helping to advise the crew and run the ship.

Saradan/Smeer was a venomous supreme commander of the Foundation, becoming foundation president and Commissioner Smeer, relentless pursuer of the rebel leader Blake, his crew, and the *Alligator*.

Crevas was an avenging Foundation space commander who was originally ordered by Saradan to locate, seek, and destroy Blake, who had injured his arm in the past.

Cartel was a strategist for the Foundation and was physically attracted to Saradan.

Counsellor Jonsen was a member of the high council of the Foundation, who ordered Saradan to kill Blake but whose ship was blown up by Saradan in a murder plot.

Krandor was a double-dealing godfather of Free City, outside Foundation control, who negotiated with Saradan but plotted behind her back in a love-hate relationship.

Ginoc was an old witch who magically created duels between enemies for sport.

Sarada was a good witch from the same planet as Ginoc, who fought duels, taking the side of goodies.

Arlen was a petty criminal and undercover Foundation officer who was captured by Blake on Gauranga when she was a bounty hunter, but she turned against the Foundation.

The Lab Masters were clones and scientists who were angelic beings and the creators of a clone of Blake for Saradan's use but who continued to help the allies due to respect of all life and later admitted to the crew of the *Phoenix* as serving under the mysterious Unmoved Mover. Kaali then suspected that the Unmoved Mover could have been referred to by the Lab Masters as the creator and source of the universe. However, the other crew remained skeptical.

Description of Fan's Sketches*
(sketches and images start overleaf)

Lab Master Sen

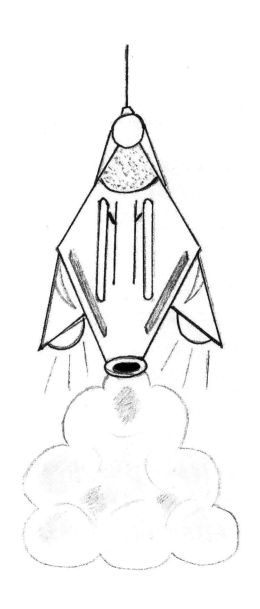

The spaceship *Phoenix* taking off

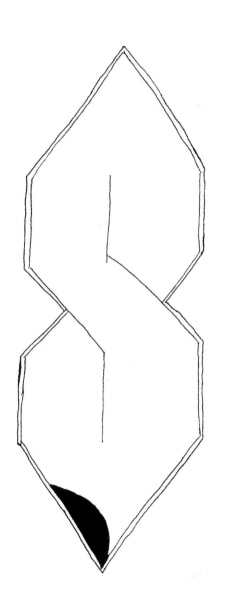

The Infinite, a sketch of a prototype
sister ship of the *Phoenix*

*Sketch 1 and 2 by Sara Sen; sketch 3 by Sacinandan K. Sen

Image of a Phoenix rising from the ashes.

Acknowledgments

The following accounts of the adventures of the Foundation rebels are inspired by the writings created by the genius late, great Terry Nation, and this is a story for all lovers of science fiction throughout the world. We are indebted to him for the extraordinary gift that he gave us through his work, which has enabled us, and many others, to view the universe from another perspective, thus subsequently broadening our minds and at the same time helping us to appreciate the qualities of humankind on this planet.

Another acknowledgment is to my father Hindole Kumar Sen as well as to Cache Creek Library and Community Futures Ashcroft, both in British Columbia, Canada, for their technical help.

This present effort is a tribute to the British actor Paul Darrow, whose acting has been the source of our inspiration. I cannot express enough of my gratitude to him.

This story is about the continuation of the life and adventures of a band of extraordinary beings who spent most of their lives in outer space on distant planets that were within the domain of a confederation and under the super state known as the Foundation planets, based and ruled from the Earth—the Foundation headquarters. The Foundation was originally a global charitable trust on Earth, but corruption and hunger for power and wealth within the trust led to the beginnings of a super state in the western world, intent on domination across the galaxies. The Foundation became too big for its own boots according to rebel groups on Earth who had to be prepared for war.

On Earth, these bold men and women faced false accusations of rebellion and treacherous activity and were falsely imprisoned, and punished by brain-washing techniques, by the Foundation authorities, from whom they were fortunately able to escape to outer space and some unchartered galaxies due to the brilliant leadership of Reg Kumar-Blake. However, some never returned alive. He was determined to fight the gross injustice inflicted upon the innocent population on Earth and other planets. He collaborated with earthlings and aliens to form a rebellious alliance.

The chief amongst their enemies in the Foundation was Supreme Commander Saradan and later Commissioner Smeer, who relentlessly pursued the rebels and planned their extinction in order to possess their advanced spaceships, the *Alligator* and later the *Skanda*.

After many battles and interactions with the popularly named "forces of darkness" scientists called the Lab Masters were able to create a clone of Kumar-Blake, at the request of Saradan (later Smeer) of the Foundation. The Lab Masters, although originally aiding Saradan, discovered that she was manipulating the use of clones for her own ends, thus breaking the scientists' rules of life. The Lab Masters also heard a rumor that Commissioner Smeer was planning to use the Lab Masters again to create a clone of herself for her own political gains. Kumar-Blake's clone would not kill for Saradan in the past and spoiled her mission, which confused and annoyed both Saradan and her ruthless and psychopathic officer Space Commander Crevas.

After many an escapade of the outlaws running from the Foundation pursuit ships and battling with Supreme Commander Saradan, Kumar-Blake and his crew were still able to prevent a complete takeover of the *Alligator* and the *Skanda* by Saradan, who had to leave after all her attempts to kill the rebels had failed. Arden had, by a mirage of a super space vehicle power threat, forced Saradan to leave the *Alligator*.

Later on the *Skanda* after Kumar-Blake's disappearance, despite feeling safer after Saradan's departure, Arden and his crew were still fighting between themselves, and had to beware of the enemy being at large in the universe. However, when the crew came to Gauranga, a cold, pale planet, they suddenly came upon a Foundation ship, face-to-face with Reg Blake, who by this time had dropped the title Kumar (meaning "prince") in his name and appeared to be a broken man with nervous exhaustion.

Arden, after being initially pleased to see Blake, suddenly remembered how Blake had abruptly left them, and listening to Brent's mistrust of Blake's intentions, he became disturbed by the thought that Blake had betrayed them, leaving them to their own destiny. Arden, with feelings of mistrust, raising his gun, asked, "Have you tricked me?"

Blake pleaded, "Arden, I was waiting for you. Can't you understand?" Then suddenly they both had their guns raised at each other. Within moments, gunshots were heard and Blake was seen lying on the deck … A further shoot-out ensued, and all the crew collapsed except Arden. It thus appeared that they were fired upon by Foundation soldiers who surrounded Arden and eventually shot him …

CHAPTER 1

The Moving Finger Writes

As the scene progressed and the entire crew of what was once the *Alligator* and the *Skanda* appeared dead, a silence lasted a few sad and tense moments, as if the universe were unable to believe that such a catastrophe had actually been perpetrated. This scene was seen millions of miles away in the most powerful of the Foundation's space stations by none other than Smeer (a.k.a. Saradan, who had miraculously survived after her forcible exit from the *Alligator*). On Earth, the chiefs of the Foundation were equally astonished and hardly able to believe that such a stroke of luck could have occurred. But this was too much of an anticlimax for the intellectual and subtle logical mind of the strategist Cartel, who was secretly admired by Smeer and who warned her to watch the turn of the events rather than actually believe the sudden shooting down of Blake and his compatriots, however real this appeared on the screen.

But the news of the unexpected demise of Blake had not only been broadcast within the boundaries of the solar system but also to far-reaching planetary systems. This was not possible without the intervention of powers hitherto unknown, a fact of great concern to the scientists of the Foundation, who were totally perplexed and felt lost about this situation.

Smeer, not knowing what to believe, kept watching the shoot-out repeatedly, but she saw that everyone appeared dead, including her secret heartthrob, Brent. Then the video that was sent to Smeer ended. Yes, it was for this attractive man that she experienced genuine feelings of love, even though she still admired the strategist. However, she called her old adversary, Krandor, to look into this unexpected incident. To her horror, she heard a voice on her communicator that she could not believe—that of Counselor Jonsen. How did he survive the explosion that she had planned herself? And now was he in a position to blackmail her should she not abide by his wishes? Smeer's world was as dark as it could be, and there was no hope for her to satisfy her strong desire to become mother to offspring by the man of her choice: Brent.

In the meantime, back on the ship on Gauranga, the Foundation soldiers, after sending the video to Smeer, took off their fake uniforms and saluted Jemma. Even Arden, whom Blake had captured when he was a bounty hunter, had changed her allegiance to Jemma without the knowledge of Blake, for the sake of secrecy. She wanted to convince Smeer that the crew was dead. Arden had only been stunned. The Foundation had been fooled! The scene of the shootings had been sent by video link to Smeer. Thinking the majority of the rebels, including Blake and Arden, had been killed, she unknowingly gave Freedom to the few left alive.

The Foundation soldiers standing among the bodies lying on the Foundation ship were working under Jemma and had also become somewhat tired of keeping up the facade for Smeer's eyes via the downloaded video link. Amidst them appeared a well-known figure standing with the Ladies of Light (the Lab Masters). This included Lab Master Sen, whose wings were covering her. Sen's quiet and confident bearing impressed Jemma!

The words "All life is together" were resounding in the commanding voice of the Lab Master. "Here endeth the first chapter," she then said, and what a glorious chapter it was. "The moving finger writes. The time has come for you to awake Arden and for all of you to arise and henceforth follow the forces of light and be guided by it."

Then the Lab Masters disappeared into thin air.

CHAPTER 2

In the Beginning Was the Word

On the ship, Arden woke up dazed. But he was even more surprised that an image was entering his mind, and he wondered if it was real. Then came the astonishment of his life: the image was not a mirage but a beautiful woman of flesh and blood standing in front of him. She was saying, "Arden, wake up. It is I, Jemma, whom you lost a long time ago. Look at me. Do I not look alive?"

Arden, now in a state of shock, blurted, "Don't tell me you are who you say you are and not a hologram. Prove, woman, that you were a member of the crew of the universe's greatest spacecraft, whose name you should be able to tell me. Otherwise, you are in trouble!"

Characteristic of Jemma, her response was sharp and to the point. She gave a quick embrace and kissed him.

That left Arden even more perplexed but certainly happier.

There was an almost uncontrollable outburst of emotions and scenes of jubilation all around, with wild embraces and laughter. "Yes, Arden," Jemma continued, "when Blake told Brent that I had blown up Foundation ships around me, he didn't know that before I hit the self-destruct button, I had teleported out. I had secretly developed a transport system, and being dead was the safest measure I could take. Even that idea I have stolen from Smeer."

Arden and his companions on the ship remained happy for a while but were somewhat perturbed by the tone of what appeared as a command by the Lab Masters rather than a commentary.

Jemma was quietly picking up the pieces in her own confident manner by giving reassurances to all the others. After her life on the

3

planet Morphenniel, she was back and things were now under control. Or perhaps a higher power had intervened in their lives in a mysterious way.

But who were these Lab Masters? And what did they want from these ordinary humans?

A new era is dawning just after time seems to have stopped, thought Arden. He could hardly resist his strong desire to rush up to Jemma and hold her in his arms. He wanted to thank her, as he was certain that she had influenced the intervention by the all-powerful Lab Masters. By their powers, they had appeared to change the scene as if on a theatre stage and give them back their lives!

Arden was brought up to look at everything around him with logical spectacles but was unable to fathom whatever was going on around him and why he was so irresistibly attracted to Jemma. Should he believe what she said about the use of a stunning device on him and not killing weapons? Above all, he did not seem able to talk about this to anyone, although he tried to make some suggestions to others on the ship that all was not as it seemed. He was skeptical even about the identity of Jemma, and this situation also perplexed Arden. Jemma's remarks worried Arden to such an extent that he decided to secretly investigate what really happened to satisfy his curiosity as to whom all these people around him truly were. Some of them seemed like complete strangers to him. He had had hardly any emotional connection with them even after so many years of association. *But what could be the starting point*, Arden thought, *if I'm unable to trust anyone?*

Even Oros could find it difficult. In any case, Arden had no idea where he could look for that computer genius. Arden was sure that something was not computing, which frustrated him. Hence, he had no alternative but to change his interrogative technique, which was not working. There was hardly any chance of anyone responding to any kind of distress signal or Mayday on his part. He realized that he was really quite helpless.

For once, he might as well take Jemma seriously and even carry out her commands for the sake of survival. But this was not the basic teaching of Charles Darwin, who had created the theory of survival of the fittest and was the man he adored as a boy while on Earth.

Jemma had definitely made her point without submitting to Arden's coercive tactics, so he let her approach him.

Jemma, holding her arm around his waist, gently started to move away from the scene. Arden was surprised he allowed himself to be guided by a woman, as he was still wondering if everything was really in his mind or if he was in a dream world where those he had seen die had risen from their mortal coil. He remembered the lines of St. John—"In the beginning was the Word"—and felt that the path of his life was predestined and probably controlled by the Logos, the Word, of the Lab Masters.

CHAPTER· 3

Escape

From his early days, Arden had always been inclined to admire the deeds of the great heroes and explorers of the ancient world. The Greek hero Odysseus was his role model, yet with the appearance of the Lab Masters, he could hardly plug his ears like Odysseus to protect himself from the singing of the sirens. Instead, Arden had to listen closely to Jemma telling him that she was alive and had no choice but to follow her plan, which she had been ordered by the Ladies of Light to carry out, with him by her side.

As Jemma now had Arden's attention, she started to speak to him in a low but firm tone of voice, saying that the entire scene of death and destruction was indeed quite unreal, as nothing like that had actually happened. "Listen," she said, "and believe that those corpses you saw were not those of the persons you knew but those of innocent clones who sacrificed their lives willingly under orders from their creators, the great Lab Masters, who have other plans for us in the map of our destiny. Yes, Arden, it was I who, unseen to all, manipulated the transport and docking systems and prevented the other hostiles from landing on this ship. The Lab Masters replaced our crew with the clones that followed you to this section, where the subsequent shooting took place. Believe also that you did not kill Blake but rather his clone. We must start our search for Blake, now that the Foundation and our enemies have been fooled by this cunning plan of Lab Master Sen."

Arden followed Jemma without question as she proceeded toward a destination where a new ship was awaiting them. To his utter surprise, holding Jemma's hands, he stepped into what appeared to be the reception of a vast and more technically advanced sanctum of a new design of space vessel. He was not slow to ascertain that this ship had been constructed for long-distance travel in deep space and was therefore ideally suited to search for Blake, the great character with whom he had a love-hate relationship in his life away from Mother Earth in his days in the *Alligator*.

Therefore, seeing a good wish message left on this new ship from the invisible Lab Masters themselves, without wasting any time, Jemma and Arden started the gigantic engine to ascend at great speed to orbit the planet of Gauranga, where they could locate the real Blake and the other compatriots by using their new and more sophisticated tractor beams to land and rescue them.

Arden managed to steer his new ship and effortlessly transport down with their advanced space suits. It was not long before he found his friend of heroic altruism lying almost frozen in a cave, along with the wreckage of the ship the *Skanda* and some of the other members of its crew as well as "Slaven," now offline, and then Arden brought the great computer with bio-intelligence, called Oros. As usual, Arden managed to control his emotions, especially happiness, as he gazed at Reg, who in turn was speechless, until they could no longer wait to express their joy in a long embrace with tears in their eyes. This surprised Jemma, who was watching from a distance with perhaps a touch of jealousy, remembering her past affection for Blake. However, Arden did not want to lose time with this unexpected success and soon responded to the warnings of the Lab Masters to get on with the difficult work of repairing the damaged circuits of Oros. Blake commenced his work of reorganizing the crew but treaded with caution while dealing with Jemma, who seemed a little distant but more in command of things than he had seen before.

Amongst the rest of the members, there was also a distinct but subtle change in behaviour, particularly on the part of Victor. He did not seem to be as cynical and skeptical about Arden's action plans as he had hitherto been. Arden attributed this to the effect of the element of shock and surprise that had overwhelmed them on recovering from the faked drama of their death created by the Lab Masters for the benefit of Commissioner Smeer in particular. In the meantime, Arden became more aware of the stern voice of the Lab Masters, who, though pleased with his success at finding Blake, were at the same time reminding him of the price that had to be paid for acquiring a truly remarkable spaceship from them. It was more advanced than the previous space vessels, matching only the *Alligator*. The price was to oust the Foundation and destroy its harmful control over the planets—at least of the solar system. Arden, Blake, and the crew knew that they would therefore have to land on Earth to continue this mission.

However, there was also another threat to the Earth, which was an asteroid heading toward the planet at great speed. Blake and the crew considered joining with some neutral experts or cooperative members of the Foundation administration. It was found that typically many of the upper echelons of the Foundation who had been associated with dictatorial Smeer in the past wanted to escape without lifting a finger to help the Earth from the impending catastrophe. Blake and the new ship's crew, having heard a distress signal from the Lab Masters about this asteroid event, had to return immediately to the Earth's atmosphere to divert the asteroid's path. The new advanced vessel allowed them to do this by the use of its weapons, such as powerful laser beams that would disintegrate large parts of the body of the asteroid, making it unstable on its axis and changing its direction away from the earth. They also provided an alternative gravitational field with gravitons that the ship was capable of producing. This had the effect of not only diverting the asteroid's path but also breaking off some parts of the big rock that fortunately hit some hostile Foundation spaceships.

Having achieved this, they then had to carry out further instructions from the Lab Masters. After toppling the dictatorship on Earth, they had to defeat any enemy armies and replace them with a people's democracy. More clones were created to help them reconstruct and repopulate the dilapidated Earth after the armies had been slain, as clones were not aggressive enough due to their philosophy that life is precious and all life is together. Blake and his crew also wanted to repopulate the Earth eventually. But as the Lab Masters had stated, Blake was ideally suited for masterminding the toppling of the evil dictatorship, as he knew the minds of such types as the venomous Smeer. In addition, no doubt Arden and the crew were past masters in their ability to predict the Foundation's responses to situations in general.

The rebel alliance was well aware that they had a race against time to re-create a peaceful life on Earth before the enemy returned.

CHAPTER 4

The Return

As Blake and the crew of the new vessel were now within the earth's orbit, they had to contend with the multiple satellites that were whizzing past them, and after much exploration and viewing of different locations from the ship, it took them some time to locate a suitable site to land. They were surprised that their landing was so uneventful, though Arden was in no doubt that it was a matter of time before the Foundation space agency detected them by satellite communication. They were not yet truly aware of the problems that they were about to encounter, having flown back to Earth after a passage of so many Earth years of being in outer space in a different time dimension. Little did they know that behind their secure landing was the mysterious power of the Lab Masters, who had been guiding them all along to planet Earth for a specific purpose: the destruction of the Foundation.

Soon after Blake and his crew found themselves on the soil of the once-distant blue planet, it was difficult for them after reaching this long sought-after goal to actually descend from their gigantic spaceship that had provided a kind of home, albeit in the far depths of outer space. It was also true that the enormous size, shape, and appearance of their vessel was probably more menacing than they reckoned, thought Victor, to the earthlings, who would be quite justified to believe that they were undoubtedly some alien beings with not so good intentions at all! In addition, who would believe that they were really humans come back to their home?

Although Victor was, as usual, warning of the impending dangers from various imaginary and probable scenarios that could be waiting for them on Earth, he had the strong inner urge to follow Blake's orders for landing preparations, while Blake and Arden started donning the special suits, the likes of which they had not seen before. In the meantime, their advanced telecommunicating instruments were recording the scenes of a great drama of a doomsday crisis seen throughout the length and breadth of the globe, and Arden and Blake wondered whether they were in the right place at all or if Victor was perhaps right that it was too risky a venture.

All this time, their spaceship, when it had orbited the Earth, was just about visible in space but was seen by the instruments of the Earth's space station as a gleaming object radiating a tremendous glow, hovering over the envelope of the Earth's atmosphere. Although beautiful, it was a frightening spectacle.

Inside, however, after Arden busied himself with the sophisticated ship telescopes, trying to get glimpses of the surface of Mother Earth through a bluish haze, he was trying to fathom in his mind as to how and where they should start their expedition. There was also the problem that this ship seemed to perform almost spontaneously, of its own volition, quite unlike the *Alligator*; even the most knowledgeable of them all, Jemma, was unable to predict or always understand what the best move was.

They had been away for some time, and Blake was suddenly ruminating on the past; he felt that the first thing that he needed to know was about the passage of time and as to what century they were currently in on Earth or how much time had elapsed since their departure from the planet. Blake was conscious of the inherent high risk of this entire mission but unable to admit this, as he was somewhat petrified of the power of the Lab Masters and the consequence of failure. He had to get as much information as possible prior to landing on the planet's surface. He also was certain that their presence had to be concealed; even sudden invisibility was an option. Hence he had to explore the technology of this procedure, and this would not be easy, as Arden had not yet been able to reconstruct Oros.

As far as the calculation of the time-dimension censor, it appeared that the current date was somewhere in the late third millennium, which was about fifty Earth years since Blake and the other members of his original group had managed to escape into the *Alligator*! This was difficult for Blake or Arden to believe, but soon the solution to their incredible and almost unsolvable mathematical problem was answered by a voice message that resounded in the air: "Yes, Blake, you have travelled back in time and will now go to the future that we have brought you here for, to help mankind and liberate them once and for all from the hands of the tyranny of the Foundation! Get yourselves ready for action—and you have our blessings!" So saying, the voice disappeared—and with it, the halo of light that was the hallmark of the Lab Masters.

Blake and Arden were somewhat perplexed and could hardly take it all in. In particular, the very thought of being time travellers was quite a shock to their rational minds, but they had no alternative but to carry out certain definite measures for landing and would no doubt ascertain the truth in the course of time anyway.

Blake and the entire team now started to get busy working with their computers while at the same time trying to listen to Arden, who was reminding them about the overall strategy of maintaining the utmost secrecy about their landing site; their identity was not to be revealed at any cost. They were strangers on this planet and must be on guard to not be caught unawares and taken prisoners.

When they started their slow descent, Blake was able to see on their screen the large domed structure of the entire city where he had previously been held captive. During their slow motion toward the surface of the Earth, the massive airship had gradually became invisible, although the NASA detectors were reporting the presence of a large unidentified alien vessel! Blake and his crew were able to hear quite clearly different Earth stations talking to each other and blaming one another for this sudden disturbance, being suspicious of each other. Hearing all the old rhetoric of false accusations left no doubt in Blake's mind that now there were different and opposing political groupings and the old Foundation had lost control as a single ruler. He would obviously have to find who and what states were aligned to each other and whose politics, if any, were to act for the benefit of humanity so that he could take sides with them. They also saw some incredible scenes of natural beauty that they thought had been wiped out, which they had somewhat forgotten.

Jemma felt that she could almost abandon everything and just settle down on a quiet corner of this planet to be a woman and nothing else. But lo! Suddenly the voice of Arden broke the silence.

"Hello, everyone. Can you hear me? Our ship has reached its destination. We have landed at last on Mother Earth—hurray! God bless what you have done! Remain where you are and await further instructions from Blake."

A chorus of voices of joy and mixed emotions filled the air while Blake stood silently in a corner. He then responded to this by raising his hands and uttering, "Thank God for all of you." It seemed that Blake had now perhaps lost all his anger against the injustice, loss, and suffering that he had to suffer previously on this planet that had once been the prime motivation for all the battles he and his crew had to fight in outer space for all this time. However, the entire station of this unique vessel seemed to light up, and the gentle but commanding voice of the Lab Masters broke the silence.

"Well done, all of you. You must now be ready for the task for which you have been chosen: to rescue the earthlings and your descendants from the rulers of the Foundation. Maintain contact with us at all times and you will overcome all obstacles on your path. Your new space suits will guide you for most of your requirements and communications. Go— and best of luck, as the earthlings say!" To the astonishment of all, the voice gradually faded away.

This left everyone in a somewhat lighter mood. Blake and Arden looked at each other and smiled, while Jemma and Victor watched them approvingly. Arden, in the meantime, had already commenced studying and demonstrating to the crew their space suits, which seemed to grow onto their bodies slowly, like new skin cells forming a shell. As Arden was getting acquainted with the different buttons on the suits, to their astonishment there was no need for them to have to dematerialize in order to be mobile or leave or return to their ship. Once they were wearing the suits, they felt that they were in complete control and could assume any form of directional motion by their will, toward the location or coordinates needed for landing on any planet. Arden made everyone realize and appreciate that these space suits were giving them mental capacities, as it were, which were much beyond what their ancestral human brains could even comprehend.

In the meantime, the crew was suddenly surprised to see that their internal monitors were no longer showing the landscape of the Arizona desert. Instead, it looked as though the ship had lifted itself and was now in the part of the earth that Arden was well familiar with—a place surrounded by the blue waters of the sea whose shores were always part of his endeared childhood memories that never faded in spite of his journeys into infinite space.

They were now in the southern landscape of England, at one time a special headquarters of the Foundation administration! However, both Blake and Arden, who had experienced life in this part of the world, had fears and a doubt as to what was awaiting them there after all these years. Of course, they were not aware that their spacecraft had already been fired upon by countless missiles of all kinds from the various defense pillboxes and rocket launchers that were fortunately being repelled by the impenetrable electromagnetic shield protecting this incredible vessel.

While looking through their sophisticated monitor screens, Blake and Arden could see that they were visualizing a well-magnified view of the earth. The vessel had moved through the outer zone of the atmospheric envelope, although some air particles were mingled within this proximity of the stratosphere. The crew was surprised to discover that meanwhile the ship had lifted and guided itself again, unlike the *Alligator* and, without Oros, had searched for a suitable location, spacious and clear enough for it to finally land and touch the soil of the Earth.

At this moment, something else happened that left both Arden and Blake completely dumbfounded. Out of nowhere, they heard a voice calling upon them to cheer up and not be afraid! It was the voice of Kaali, who was now standing before them and laughing. "I am real, Blake, not a ghost, and I have been sent back to you in a different time vortex. Maybe Jemma will explain to you presently."

It was a shock, but somehow both the men seemed to be able to accept this situation, as if happy that this telepath from the planet Avon, which had such mental powers that had assisted them in a many a tight corner before, had now come to help them again in their perhaps most tricky venture—what the crew hoped would be the final clash with Smeer and the Foundation.

Kaali, of course, was once again in action and, holding on to Jemma, went swiftly into a meditative trance to try to fathom what was in store for them before entering into a deeper state. She kept saying in a low tone of voice, "Blake, beware, beware of the humans. They are not what they seem—hypocrisy exists everywhere!" Kaali continued in this voice, anxiously muttering, "Listen, the Lab Masters are talking to me. They are saying that according to the rule of life created by the Unmoved Mover, we are meant to only live permanently on our own planets or we will die earlier … They want a mission to be fulfilled—to raise a strong new generation on another planet, then return them to Earth to wipe out dictatorships there before they weaken with age."

Arden did not seem to take heed of these warnings, or whatever they really signified, as he was a believer in rational deduction rather than intuitive knowledge, and as such, he tended to ignore much of what she tried to impart as vital information.

Blake, on the other hand, seemed to be able to accept this dark side of Kaali and took her observations quite seriously, agreeing with her that they would have to proceed with extreme caution, as the earthlings were still in the grip of a ruthless and totalitarian control that operated throughout the world and through all its nation states. Blake, more than Arden, felt that they had to use their resources with careful planning rather than depend upon the artificial intelligence of a computer like Oros.

Arden, in turn, had vital information, which he tried to tell all, that any data could be made available from a universal computer that could be contacted by pressing upon a disk which was attached to their highly technically advanced space suits.

On the ship monitor, they saw green fields, a cathedral, and a town in the distance.

Victor remarked, "Well, that's great, isn't it? After all these years, maybe there's no one to meet us."

Arden replied somewhat sarcastically, "Victor, firstly, if they were here to meet us, they would kill us; and secondly, this ship is on a setting to make itself invisible to all earthlings and radar at this time. All they can probably see is a hole in the landscape."

Jemma asked, "Where are we?"

Kaali, using her mental powers, said, "We are at … I think it's called … Wait a second … Warm … Warminster—in what was known as Wessex, now Wiltshire. Yes, that's the cathedral over there."

Blake commented softly, "In the old days, around the twentieth century, this was the most popular place for UFO sightings."

Kaali said, "We don't have much time."

The voice of the Lab Masters, along with a light, appeared in the ship. They said loudly, "Do not be afraid. Be bold, go forth, and explore this place. We will speak into your minds about your next moves once you have left this ship. Remember, the Unmoved Mover wants you to fulfill this task for which you have been brought back for, into the time of the cosmos that still had the Foundation on Earth. To arrive here, you travelled through one of the gigantic wormholes in the space-time fabric of this galaxy."

They stepped cautiously out of the ship and walked across the green landscape wearing their space suits, which contained their armory and invisibility devices. Jemma, however, decided to stay behind, as she remembered that in the past, Blake would entrust her to remain in the *Alligator* at the controls and maintain contact with him while he explored and assessed the situation on the ground.

Arden was somewhat silent, as he could not yet fathom as to whether they were truly invisible, although he noticed the absence of any earthlings as he and Blake and the crew walked out of the massive and invisible door of the ship. They seemed to be guided by a beam of light that looked like a powerful laser pencil of light shining over the green patch of English soil that they were now treading upon. *Indeed,* thought Arden, *how fortunate we are in spite of all that we have gone through. Our luck has turned this way, and we are once again on the lap of Mother Earth after so many years—still so alive and young!* He felt a kind of strange gratitude and respect for Blake, without for whose courage and longing for justice, he would not have experienced the kind of life that helped him open his inner eye and see the world through a different angle than mere self-centeredness and material gain. It was as if he was born again and his vision was now greatly magnified. He was astonished that he had in the past depended so much on Oros, a computer, to make important decisions and to influence him as much as it did. He had almost lost his human emotions and had made errors of judgement in developing any relationships, but now, to his surprise, the sight and smell of flowers on the soil of the English countryside suddenly brought back memories of his childhood. He felt human all over again and for once felt genuinely closer to all the crew with whom he had been with for all these years in time and space.

In the meantime, the Earth censors all over the globe were recording an unexplainable phenomenon of a "gap" in the landscape, and radio and TV broadcasts were asking the populations to remain patient, as the forces of the Foundation were about to deal with "aliens" from Mars or anywhere nearby as soon as they were caught in the detectors on land or by telescopes and satellites in space. Were these his feelings? Or was he taken over by a controlling mind—possibly of the Lab Masters? Given the euphoria that he was sensing, it was a feeling that was hard to resist. He suddenly decided to do a full blood count and full blood biochemistry analysis on himself. The results of the analysis seemed normal, so he couldn't have been drugged either.

CHAPTER 5

The Phoenix

While getting a broad picture of the events taking place on Earth, where it seemed that the old center of control of the Foundation had eventually disintegrated, it was difficult for Blake or Arden to fathom whether the same group of people who had controlled their lives before were still in some concealed location in the Southeast of England, such as in or around the vast city of London. But there were definite pictures in the sensor screens of groups of armed militia still walking around in the streets of towns and cities, although the countryside was still almost empty and dark.

Arden suddenly heard some conversations in the audio monitors that led him to believe that quite a number of people were hiding in tunnels such as the underground transport system he had once known in some Earth cities. He had another shock when he heard a voice speaking to him: "Whoever you are, we do know you are from another world in space, but so are we. We are not ghosts but are hiding in the Tower of London, waiting for rescue from the hands of modern executioners who not only want our heads but are also slowly taking over the entire world. Do not be mistaken that all is well in London.

There were other voices: "Hello out there from us in Starcross, in South West England. We call ourselves the Starcrusians, a group from here who wants to flee to a neutral planet. The countryside here is dark and desolate here. Please help us—the River Exe is slowly covering us!"

Other pleas came through on the monitors: "Hello, mariner from outer space. Our royals have gone, and our parliament is nonexistent. Reserves in the city are not going to last long. Have you come to help us or can you pick us up in your vessel to finally escape from this planet? Even the ghosts from the tower want to leave with us."

The old prophecies turned out to be quite accurate. Kaali was able to perceive the number of invisible aliens who had brought about the collapse of the kingdoms around the world (unknown to man but sometimes seen as unidentified flying objects.) In spite of great vigilance and organizations tracking down these aliens, the internal conflicts between the groups of nations taking on a religious dimension divided the old united Foundation. This consisted of a Western bloc of Christian- and Islamic-based states and a powerful Mongolian group that consisted of ancient Chinese. These were all now at conflict. It seemed apparent to many that the heating of the planet was also contributing and making it imperative that the ultimate rescue would be for these powerful groups to resolve their differences and prepare for leaving the earth by interplanetary space travel to other dimensions.

Arden, however, was suspicious of both the voices from the tunnel and the radio signals from the Tower of London. He thought, *Are they hoaxes to try to bait the crew in? Are they really working for the old Foundation?* Arden asked, "Kaali, do you think these are traps?"

Kaali murmured, "Give me some time. I have to think of each of them in turn. I'm getting mixed messages … Let me rest and then I will tell you."

While Kaali was resting, Arden overheard the memorable name Anson repeatedly coming from the tunnel. He told Blake. Then Blake replied in a frustrated and confused tone, "But Anson was killed when we rescued Oros."

Arden impatiently said, "We can transport to the tunnels and find out."

Victor quickly snapped, "Why would any of us have to risk our necks to find out?"

Blake and Arden just looked at Victor as if to say, *Victor, you haven't changed!*

Kaali then put a voice in the head of Blake. "I think it's all right. He is related to the original Anson, so we may need him …"

Blake said, "Yes, we may need him for support to recolonize a new planet—a planet for a rebel force to exist upon—a rebel planet."

"Listen, we don't just need him for that; we need him to reconstruct Oros!" Arden remarked.

Anna asked, "How are we going to get into the tunnels?"

Blake replied, "Victor will help open the doors. We'll have to blast ourselves in."

Victor remarked, while taking a flask of soma, "Now look—that might scare them, and they might think we are the enemy."

While pushing Victor's flask aside, Arden shouted, "Victor, there are no excuses left! Let's go!"

Kaali just got up from resting, joined the others, and said, "What about the Tower of London?"

Blake replied, "We can deal with them afterward. Maybe Brent can go later with Anna and Sara. Come to think of it, where is Brent?"

Kaali said, dazed, "There's no time. We must get people out of the tunnel first … I don't know why, exactly."

"Because it will be an advantage to us—that's why!" replied Arden.

Jemma worked the transport for Blake Arden and Victor. She brought Anson and some scientists and doctors back to the ship. Anson's son (not Anson, they discovered) was amongst them. She could only bring a few people in invisible suits. Anson's son, called Anson II, had already started to build a new and smaller version of Oros, which had a female voice that reminded him of his late wife. Arden claimed that version for himself, in exchange for some jewels.

Anson helped rebuild the older Oros. They decided to use both versions on the invisible ship, a ship in the shape of a bird, which Anna and Sara called the *Phoenix*. They termed it this because it was like a bird that rose from the ashes of all the dead rebels who helped them against the Foundation in the "old days." The Lab Masters had engineers who knew about invisible space travel at tachyon speed, a speed beyond the speed of light. After all, this was the technology of the Lab Masters, and Anna and Sara worked with Jemma to complete the design of the *Phoenix*, which could travel faster and more discreetly through outer space even better than the *Alligator*.

The functioning of the transport system did take time to fathom, especially for Victor. They not only had transport bracelets and space suit disks but another active and safer way of teleporting that they could use on hostile planets, where bracelets could be stolen or looted from the crew. Of course, the rebel crew had to use their instincts, assisted by Kaali, to deduce which transport technology to use on which planet.

It was also heard through rebel space communications that any being should beware of a virus that was given to some captured rebels

Sara L Sen

by the Foundation. The virus gave the effect of painful shocks all over the body due to extreme inflammation subsequently pinching nerves and activation of glutamate-aspartate neurotransmission. They therefore took anti-inflammatory and antispasmodic drugs before landing.

CHAPTER 6

The Mysterious Passenger

The crew knew they had to search for Brent, but first they picked up some people in the Tower of London and dropped them on the surface of their new rebel planet. They had found the planet with their ship sensors.

In the meantime, Brent was in the shattered remains of what was known as Paris, on the top of the still-existing Eiffel Tower. This structure was used as a communications tower by the powers on the planet. As the *Phoenix* approached the Eiffel Tower, the sun appeared to set and be replaced by an unidentified gap in the landscape. The crew saw a figure who looked like Brent on their visual display, with someone who resembled Commissioner Smeer of the Foundation in his arms. "Is it Brent?" the crew asked. Yes, from his birthmark, it clearly was. Victor remarked that it definitely was, as he had a woman in his arms.

As the ship's sensors homed in on the woman, they were not sure if it was Smeer. Arden had another shock. Could she be alive but still young?

Blake said, "Don't be too sad, Arden; I'm sure that she's not the woman you had a soft spot for. It was years ago that you were taken in by Saradan's charm, when you were stuck on that planet together.

Arden showed annoyance but realized that there was a grain of truth in this. Arden listened in more closely to hear the voices of Brent and the mysterious woman. To his utter surprise, he heard that she was talking in the same tones that reminded him of Saradan; the woman uttered to Brent that she was attracted to him ever since she saw some old video footage of him with Saradan. Arden saw the couple embracing, at which point he decided to speak to Brent through the communicator in Brent's space suit.

"For God's sake, Brent, come back to the ship, with or without her, for your own safety. And Smeer, if you are with her, will certainly get old quickly if she stays in the earth's atmosphere, for she broke the rule of life. This is what the Lab Masters say."

Brent and the woman teleported back to the ship. "Let me introduce …," Brent began, but the woman interrupted him.

"No, I will not say my name at this point. However, I will tell you that I am the daughter of Smeer, alias Saradan."

That night, Kaali had some disturbed thoughts and confided in Jemma. "It seems as if this woman wants to take over the ship and use Arden for information—and later Brent as a slave."

Arden overheard this, and the next morning, he tried to drug Smeer's daughter with a truth drug in her food. The plan failed when the crew later saw her emerging from the ship's restroom full of energy. The crew, except Brent, surrounded her in silence. Brent emerged from a restroom and walked behind this strange woman, who then grabbed Brent and forced one of the ship's weapons to his neck.

Jemma shouted, "Okay, let's say you kill Brent. Go ahead. Don't you think we could make a better deal? You can go free with him; it's his choice. We can leave the solar system to you and your criminals. Don't forget, the Lab Masters are watching. They have tremendous powers. Anyway, what good is a ship when you can have the Earth back?"

Suddenly, the ship started moving at top speed. Jemma had preset the controls when she saw this woman coming in. She smelled trouble. This caused at least enough distraction to help the crew grab the woman and try to transport her into outer space; however, she overcame the transport controls and teleported herself back to a space station nearby.

On this space station, Smeer's daughter entered an office. "I am s-sorry, Mother," she stammered, looking at the figure sitting at the desk. Don't worry; I will make sure the earth will be back in the right hands. It's just a case of the right time. I will need to stay with you here for a while. You know that I've never let you down in my life."

There was an indifferent and callous reply. "You don't have much time then, do you?"

CHAPTER 7

Victor and the Rise of Crew Morale

Up until now, Victor felt resigned to tolerate the dark emotions plaguing the crew of the *Phoenix*, but he knew that this situation had to be changed. Sara was trying to prop up the courage of Blake, but the crew knew that this was a feeble attempt. "Blake" Sara said softly, "I remember when my father told my four-year-old brother not to kiss his mother because she was 'unclean.' This was because she was committing adultery, but as innocent youngsters, not understanding the meaning of my father's statement, we asked our mother, "Have you taken a bath?"

Puzzled, Blake looked up, and asked, "Really? And what is the moral of this story?"

"It means that you may not be ready for what the Lab Masters are telling you, but must develop yourself to understand and trust them that this will pay off in the future."

There was no response to Victor's musings today. In fact, there was silence amongst the crew.

Victor scoffed, "You can cut the atmosphere in here with a knife."

In an attempt to change the mood of the crew, Victor continued. "How many Lab Masters does it take to change a light bulb?" The crew looked over and sighed in response. "Nobody?" Victor asked.

Blake replied sarcastically, "None. They just ask me to do that."

The crew looked perplexed but then smiled. Victor switched on Oros, whom Victor had programmed to tell jokes and riddles. Oros, in an enthusiastic tone, asked, "How many Lab Masters does it take to change and rejuvenate a tired old disgruntled Blake? Anybody?"

The crew laughed and said, "Yes, yes," rolling their eyes.

Victor replied, "Get Victor to do that!"

However, Oros continued, almost interrupting Victor. "How many Lab Masters does it take to change the morale aboard the *Phoenix*?"

Victor replied quickly, pointing his finger. "None—too many free radicals. Ha!" He slapped his thigh.

Oros had been programmed with the explanation of the joke and proceeded to explain the meaning. "Free radicals can mean rebels who are free but radical in their social context and behaviour.Free radicals are also termed as chemical entities with one unpaired electron that contributes to aging in man. What a marvellous pun!"

"Yes, marvellous," Jemma said disinterestedly, moving away to check her flight computers. "You could take that joke on the road."

Arden, interjecting, continued Jemma's sentence. "Just don't come back."

Victor said, "Now look … Oh, Oros, never mind." Victor smiled and took a glass of liquid sedative back to his ship quarters. "Victor is victorious," he said to himself.

CHAPTER 8

Colonization of New Planets

The Lab Masters got in touch with the space station. "Smeer and daughter, this is Lab Master Sen. This is a warning. If you colonize Earth again, you will age very quickly. Since you made a clone of Blake many Earth years ago, you broke the rules of life so many times. Therefore, we now have the power to speed up your aging process on this planet if you try to colonize it again for greed and killing."

Lab Master Sen added further, "However, we have heard that the witch Ginoc, on a planet not far from here, is bringing a situation of war again, just for her entertainment and sport. You have someone else coming to your space station at this moment who will contribute to this war."

A figure pounded the walls outside. Smeer's daughter opened the door to the office. A large figure walked in slowly and approached the desk.

"Saradan, or Smeer, or whoever you are, this is your old associate."

There was silence.

"Yes, it is Crevas."

Further shock rent the air. Smeer asked, "Is this you or is this a reconstruction before me?"

"You could say so. I survived after being thrown into outer space. I don't know how, but the old witch Ginoc rescued me. The cyber surgeon helped repair my arm and rebuilt my eye. I then stole a ship, went to Earth, and befriended people in the Tower of London. This got me access to the new ship that your daughter has just visited."

"So," Smeer interrupted, "Blake and his crew are definitely together on this new ship?"

Crevas replied, "Yes, your daughter is not wrong. This ship has an invisibility device. I hid amongst people who were teleported up to their ship. I think they call it the *Phoenix*. I then stole a pod from their ship and left in it when they were distracted."

Smeer interjected slyly, "I actually don't care how you are still alive, Crevas. However, I am a bit curious. Tell me."

"Why should I?" Crevas answered, sarcastically. "Anyway, all I will say is that it has something to do with somehow arriving on a planet after being kicked off a ship by Blake's 'fearless' rebels years ago and coming before the old hag again, who said that she saved me with her powers, as she wanted more battles for her entertainment."

Smeer added, "You no longer work for me, Crevas. I have more successful associates now."

Crevas exited the office and went back onto his small pod. He had in mind another planet to visit …

The crew of the *Phoenix* arrived for a second time at the new rebel planet to drop more rescued people from Earth onto the surface. It was a desolate landscape but had a livable climate. Blake thought that it was a suitable place to raise a new generation, after which they would all return to Earth to continue their fight for freedom and sustain peace. It was a plan at least, especially bearing in mind the words of the Lab Masters. As Anna was saying goodbye to the group and the other crew were not far away carrying out a quick exploration, she was grabbed from behind and thrown to the floor.

"Remember me?"

Anna froze. "Crevas? That voice is familiar. Well?"

When the rest of the crew realized Anna was not with them, Kaali remembered her doubts about one person in the rescued group who looked suspicious but disappeared from the ship before they all teleported onto this planet's surface. Had that person come back to the planet? She thought so intensely about this that she passed out.

Blake turned around. "Anna," he moaned, "please keep calm."

Crevas, holding his arm around her neck, shouted and laughed. "Well, crew, great to see you. Ginoc has instructed me to take this lovely lady back to her planet. I might be back."

He took her to the stolen pod and disappeared. Everything seemed to shake on liftoff, causing everyone to fall to the ground.

With head in hands, Blake said, "Let's go."

As soon as the crew, minus Anna, arrived back on the ship, Arden and Blake stood facing one another. The ship was still in the planet's orbit.

Sara walked past them. "What's going on?" she asked in a despondent tone. "Things have gone mad—and who are these Lab Masters, anyway?"

On hearing this, Blake's and Arden's eyes widened at the same time, though no one noticed.

Blake muttered in a tone of realization, "I had a dream when we all last slept. I asked the Lab Masters who they thought they were disrupting our lives like this. They said they were only messengers from a higher power that values human life and their relationships even above their own power. They also said that as Lab Masters, they were not capable of love, only creating what has been instructed for them to do. They said that evil only exists so that all beings can know the difference between selflessness and selfishness; however, all beings are only able to leave their own planets and survive under the power of their leader. I asked who the higher power is. They said that humans are simultaneously one with and different from it—and all will be revealed if we followed Lab Master Sen's message of instruction—that this power wants us to fulfil our mission of sustaining life and the power of human relationships, as it is the only way to defeat the Foundation."

Arden said, "I had … the same dream … as well."

There was suddenly a soft light with different colours coming through the portholes of the ship. A strange sensation came over Blake and Arden, which seemed to force them, against their will, to grasp each other by their arms in a manner of comradeship. They were both stunned. The coloured lights outside left the ship, and they both pulled out of their grasp, not fully aware of what just happened.

Was it an absence? Arden thought for a nanosecond. "Well," said Arden, trying to appear to be indifferent. "It was a dream telling of message of human weakness, nothing more."

"Yes, and the Lab Masters haven't been through what I've been through all this time. What do they know?"

Kaali sent a mind message to Blake and Arden, saying, "Come off it. You both enjoyed that comrades-in-arms moment, didn't you?"

"I have a proposal," Arden said softly.

"That's funny—so did I," Blake said.

Arden continued. "If you take me with the 'female' Oros to Free City, on that planet that we used to go to for a fun night out, then I will not darken your door again."

"Could you drop me there too?" Victor said.

"Okay, before I answer that, let me say my proposal. Jemma and I want to colonize a new planet," Blake said excitedly.

"Well, why don't you transport back to the planet we just left, for a while, and see what it's like?" Arden replied.

Blake said, "Agreed."

Jemma and Blake were returned to the planet's surface with Arden's expert piloting. When they arrived, Jemma said, "Blake, don't you think we should be asking someone else about this?"

Blake replied in a surprised tone. "You mean ask the Lab Masters for permission to colonize a planet that is already free for the taking?"

Jemma interjected. "Well, Blake, they do have extraordinary powers."

"But how do we ask them, Jemma?" Blake replied in a frustrated tone.

Before they could continue, a voice seemed to come out of a light in the sky. "Yes, you may, Blake. We know you are not immortal. We expected this question from you. However, you will have to pay a price. You must give the ship to Arden—he might be of future use to us."

They continued before Blake could interrupt. "Remember, Blake, that we are not just Lab Masters as you see us. We are descendants of higher beings who work under the instruction of the great unknown transcendent being—the Unmoved Mover—of all things for all time. We are here to see that life is kept reverent. Our leader tells us that being mindful of beings having 'simultaneous social unity and diversity' is the key to freedom and success. Just look at the diversity even in your human personality; see the ditherers like Brent, the cowards like Victor, or the skeptics like Arden. Let them be who they are, but work together for the same purpose of fighting corruption. No matter how revengeful you feel, this is not just your fight and you must consider others during your mission. We are told that even evil exists as a test so that our leader sees that the common beings realise the difference between right and wrong. We Lab Masters, in our a quest for using science for survival of life, have been told that we will become immortal, living with the Unmoved Mover, who stands for respect for life and freedom. Blake, do not be ashamed of your mixed race or physical condition. You have been given the special mission to unite life to fight for righteousness, of which you will know the meaning when you will ally with our leader, who has the ultimate power. The Unmoved Mover needs you too, Blake. Now, be proud to call yourself Blake-Kumar again and break out of the oppression that the Foundation has created throughout the cosmos!"

Blake was quite moved that he had been forgiven for not being able to fulfill the entire mission of replacing the Foundation. However, his partial success and his present motivation to fulfill his own life were now being accepted.

Blake and Jemma decided to say goodbye to Arden, who dropped them onto the new earth-like rebel planet, where human life could at last attempt to survive …

Thus ended the adventures of the partnership of two brave men—Blake and Arden—who risked their lives against the Foundation, along with the crew. The person who was most pleased was Jemma, who was looking forward to mothering Blake's offspring and colonizing the planet.

Blake watched the *Phoenix* take off. Little did Blake know that his opting out from further adventures in space was not looked upon kindly, in particular by Kaali and Sara.

Brent was confused and was secretly contemplating a plan to see Saradan's daughter again. Nor was the crew willing to accept Arden's command of the *Phoenix* (as they would have to subdue their instincts of settling down in one place) to go with him to make a final mission to find Anna.

Arden, seeing Blake seeking new progeny and feeling a little lonely at times, did for a moment contemplate having a son who could continue his own wishes; however, he had to resist these thoughts for the sake of freedom of movement in space. Kaali, with her sixth sense, knew that they would shortly meet up with their partners, depending on the plans of the Lab Masters. Kaali suspected that the mysterious Unmoved Mover could have been referred to by the Lab Masters as the creator and source of the universe. The other crew, however, remained skeptical.

Once in space, Arden was quite happy, but inwardly he was planning to find a wormhole through which he could traverse large distances in a short time and maybe one day reach the star system of Proxima Centuri, approximately four light years from Earth. Arden suddenly took control of the ship and left the orbit of the planet. "I'm sure that they will be happy there with a new rebel group," he said to himself with a chuckle.

The other crew angrily shouted and struggled with Arden. They couldn't face Arden putting their lives in his hands, let alone making all the decisions. Arden knocked out both Kaali and Sara. Brent was also struck down onto the deck after a longer struggle. Arden was now left alone … or was he? Victor hid in the bowels of the ship, still hoping for a free ride to Free City.

Arden, unknown to the other crew, looked at the newly reconstructed Oros, laughed, and said to himself, "From now on, it's Free City, then the universe!"

The End (and a new beginning)

Afterword

Blake and Jemma's son on Earth clashed with Smeer's daughter and started a new rebellion on earth. The remaining crew of the *Phoenix* still traveled with Arden, but with caution. However, Victor also arrived at Free City with Arden but stole Oros from him and eventually formed a comedy duo.

There was no doubt that order was gradually winning over chaos and the invisible hand of the powerful beings in this story was still supporting the rebels (including Arden on the *Phoenix*), who were still struggling, in their own way, to restore peace on earth and goodwill amongst men.

Kaali later speculated that the Lab Masters could be the angelic servants of the creator of the universe—whom most earthlings called the Creator. She then contemplated the messages of these angelic beings and wondered if she would grow old quickly unless she returned to her planet Avon. But who would be there to live with her? Would she be long-lived yet alone, making it a bad move for her? She still had many questions in her mind.

The story does not quite end here, as the saga keeps on slowly unfolding and further generations seek examples from heroic rebels like Blake and Arden and make further attempts in their lifetimes to reach an ideal that is difficult to accomplish in practice (like the adventures of *The Iliad*, which inspired generations of humans to achieve a better world.)

The Lab Masters, at least, were on the rebel's side. Smeer disappeared from the space station. They found out later that she was killed, but by whom? Was this just another rumor?

Blake had a new planet from which to teach a new uprising.

Brent, despite his initial feelings for Smeer's daughter, still hid from her, as he heard a rumor of the Foundation council that she had killed her mother over a jealous argument over him.

The rebel planet grew in inhabitants. Arden designed a prototype for a new *Phoenix II* for the future, as a disguise to use against any pursuit ships.

Blake became less ashamed to use his name Kumar-Blake, for which he was previously persecuted, and found the technology of cloaking/invisibility devices. He started to develop technology with the intent to use it to cloak the whole planet so that it would turn into something that the evil powers thought did not exist, as in the case of Star Dust many years ago. This would be for their protection. Blake called it Project Star Dust, after their proposed name of the planet Star Dust. This name of a star was also meant to protect the planet itself, as it was not a star at all. But how long before the ones who lacked respect for life would find their planet? It was a risk the rebel forces would have to take …

About the Author

Dr. Hindole Sen, a medical doctor and neuropsychiatrist for forty years in the UK, and his daughter Sara Sen, the author, along with her siblings Anna and Jon were fans of British sci-fi in the late seventies. Sara was only eight years old at the time but grew up to be a laboratory biomedical research scientist, and with Hindole later learned to appreciate the science within the fiction, particularly being inspired by the work of Terry Nation and the academic neuroscience work of Chris Boucher.

Sara (while retiring from work in the laboratory) knew that stories in the same style of Nation's and Boucher's creative works could live on, and she thought that with her father's support, she could write this story as a gift, for herself, the family, and fellow science fiction fans of all ages.

Hindole, who inspired Sara to be an author and publish this work, is retired and living in the UK. Sara currently resides in an eco-village in British Columbia, Canada, with her husband, Paul. Working as a health consultant, she tries to emulate the respect for life and a simpler health-conscious lifestyle—a philosophy also put forth by the characters the Lab Masters in this work.